The Emperor's Gift

by Gertrude Weaver

illustrations by Unada

THOMAS NELSON & SONS

Author's Note

The Emperor's Gift is based on the few known facts concerning the discovery of silk in China about 2700 B.C. It is believed to have been discovered by the Empress of China during the dynasty in which Huang-Ti was Emperor. The Empress has been called by several names similar to Si Ling Chi—the one used in this story. It is generally conceded that she did invent the loom on which the silk threads were woven, and that the Chinese word for silk—*si*—is so called for her. The English word "silk" is traced by some to the Chinese word *si*.

"Si"—Chinese character for "silk"

Contents

1

Ta Lo's Wonderful Child

Ta Lo was in a state of near desperation. This was not good. He was High Counselor to the Emperor of all China and the Emperor of all China was only five years old, learning his lessons but still willful and more interested in play than in the problems of state and governing. What made it so bad for Ta Lo was that the young Emperor Huang-Ti scarcely allowed Ta Lo out of his sight. Ta Lo was the closest person to the young Emperor. His father had died in a hunting accident two years ago. His mother had died when he was born. He had no brothers. If he had ever had sisters they had long since been removed to other houses since they were unimportant to his life and no woman was permitted to influence him.

Of course, someday he would have to choose a wife, and
this Ta Lo would have to supervise, but that was a long
time away and he did not have to think about it on
this terrible day.

Terrible day! Terrible day! And it was all the fault of
his fourth wife, scarcely more than a child herself,
taking three days to bring forth his child. No baby should
take that long in coming! It was also the fault of his
oracle, Poco Shan, who had lost all his wisdom and his
magic and couldn't tell him definitely what this fourth
baby was going to be. For months he had been asking if
this one was going to be a son, and always the same
uncertain answer from Poco Shan, always the future
had been obscure and too dim to see. Now the baby
was being born, and even this morning Poco Shan
could only give evasive answers.

Surely, the child had to be a son. Surely, after having
four wives and three girl children, this one had to be
his wonderful son. Poco Shan said the child would
be wonderful but he couldn't say whether it would be
a son. But of course it had to be a son or it would not
be wonderful. Ta Lo shook his head and smiled.
Of course, it would be his son, his wonderful son.

He would put that young Emperor in a happy frame
of mind by letting him ride his pony with the stablemaster
and he would slip over to his own household to see
if the child had yet arrived.

But Huang-Ti was the Emperor, sacred person of the
whole empire whose wish was law, and he did not want
to ride with the stablemaster this terrible day.

"Ta Lo, I want to go with you to your house to help you
welcome your new son. You are sure it will be a son?"

"No, no. Your sacred person can never enter any but
your own palace," cried Ta Lo. "And yes, yes, only
a son could be a wonderful person. Now I must hurry
to greet him."

"Don't go, Ta Lo! Don't leave me," cried the Emperor.
"Ta Lo, I can't bear for you to love this new son so much.
Don't go without me." Huang-Ti flung his arms about
Ta Lo's legs and wept and wailed.

"It is not permitted for you to go with me. The
soldiers would throw me in the dungeon if I were to try
to take you. Then neither of us could welcome my son.
Be a big fellow and write my son a greeting while I am
gone. Perhaps you will want to send a gift with the
message. You can think about this while I am gone."

"Oh, I would like that," cried the boy Emperor, jumping to his feet. "I will prepare such a message while you are gone."

"And you will know my son is born when I ring the great golden bell I have bought for this occasion and have never yet rung because I have so far had three daughters and never a son. It is the great sorrow of my life."

Because Ta Lo was Chief Counselor to the Emperor his home and estates were next to the royal palace, separated only by a high stone wall. The distance was not great because it was very necessary that the Chief Counselor be available to the Emperor at all times. Now Ta Lo quickly mounted his horse and sped homeward. He urged his already swift horse to go even faster and whirled into his household still feeling like the wind. He was smiling brightly, but it was not a happy atmosphere he entered.

"Where is everyone?" he shouted. "Where is this wonderful new child? Where is my son?" But no one came running. His three daughters had hidden behind a large screen in the main hall just outside the bedroom where the doctor and nurse were hovering over his young wife. Poco Shan sat on his heels muttering prayers.

Ta Lo entered, shouting at him.

"What have you to tell me, Poco Shan? Has the baby been born? Are you able to tell me that I have a son?"

Poco Shan fell on his knees before Ta Lo. "Oh, strong, wise Counselor, bear with your poor oracle who still cannot see clearly what the child is that is not yet born and is fighting to take hold of life."

"What!" shrieked Ta Lo. "And you dare to call yourself an oracle! You are a disgrace to your famous father, the greatest oracle in China! Do I not pay you well, Poco Shan, for your services? Have you not known for months that this household has been expecting a baby? Have I not asked you to learn from the gods what this child would be?"

"Indeed and indeed!" cried Poco Shan bowing very low.

"Then, numbskull, sit down on that stool. Put on your great silly thinking hat, and tell me what this child will be. I have spent much money on a golden bell to ring if a son is born. I want to know what it will be so that I can start ringing the bell now if it is a son."

The soothsayer was very conscientious. He had followed his father's careful teachings and had spent hours consulting the gods. He knew that he had a very

good answer for Ta Lo if he would only listen. The three sisters behind the screen were to remember what he said then many years later.

In fear and confusion, Poco Shan spoke. "Great Counselor, most wise advisor to the Emperor, ring the golden bell, for the child about to be born will be greatly honored and greatly loved by all China. The child will be famous beyond your fondest dreams, but I cannot see clearly that it will be a son."

Ta Lo grew really angry. He shook both fists and jumped up and down, screaming at the oracle. "Stupid, deceitful, incompetent soothsayer! Cheap fortuneteller! Rogue! How can the child be so great, so famous, and not be a son? Answer me that."

"But, Your Honor, I cannot answer you that because it is a great mystery surrounded in darkness. I report to you what my most careful inner ear has heard from all the household gods."

"Then I will tell you," shouted Ta Lo, pushing Poco Shan off the high stool and knocking off his magician's tall hat. "The child could only be a son, a manchild of great intelligence and courage. I shall go and ring the golden bell myself and shout the happy news to all of China." And Ta Lo did run out to ring the golden bell.

Meanwhile, Huang-Ti, the boy Emperor, waiting in his palace, alone except for a bodyguard who never let him out of his sight, had decided to give a jade box to Ta Lo's new son. This jade box had been made for Huang-Ti's father by a great artist. The artist had very cleverly cemented the jade with sandlewood so that the two elements, wood and stone, looked like one. Slivers of jade of various colors had been set in the wood to make the wood carvings into lovely pictures, and the box had been perforated throughout with a sharp instrument dipped in gold. This unusual box had been made to hold a nightingale, a gift for the Emperor. The bird had been removed to a suitable cage, but the box with its interesting secret compartments remained a beautiful and lasting ornament. It had no great interest for Huang-Ti, but he knew it would please Ta Lo, who had always admired the box.

But when he heard the golden bell ringing joyously, his feelings were all mixed up. "Ta Lo has his son!" he shouted. "Ta Lo has his wonderful son!" Then without knowing why, the boy Emperor burst into tears.

"You are in pain?" asked the bodyguard. "I should call a servant? I should call the physician?"

"No, no, no!" shouted Huang-Ti, embarrassed that anyone should see him in tears. "That bell ringing means that Ta Lo has a wonderful son. Ta Lo will love his wonderful son more than he loves me. I do not want him to love another son more."

The bodyguard was required to protect the Emperor's life, but this was a lonely little boy crying. He offered what comfort he could.

"Your Great Imperial Highness," he said bowing, "all the people in China love you as they do their own families, and Ta Lo will not love his son more."

The boy Emperor smiled and returned to the difficult task of writing a greeting to Ta Lo's new son:

> Greetings, small one! I am Huang-Ti, your
> Emperor. I send you this jade box to hide
> your dreams in. May it bring you joy.

This was a very long message for a small boy, and his bodyguard had to help him several times. When he was finished, he called a servant and asked him to take the gift and message to Ta Lo's household. Then he fell asleep.

The messenger arrived just as Ta Lo was about to re-enter his house after ringing the bell. He wore a wide smile as he met the messenger and bowed very low as he accepted the gift. The messenger departed and Ta Lo entered the house. Placing the gift upon a beautiful table, he turned around to see the faces of the doctor and the nurse. They were not happy. The nurse, holding the baby, did not look up.

Ta Lo stepped back, his eager smile vanishing. "My son has died!" he cried. "My hopes of an heir do not live! Why have you let this child die?" he screamed at the doctor.

"Ta Lo, Counselor to the Emperor, the child has not died. It is a beautiful, most healthy infant, but the baby is a girl."

"What?" screamed Ta Lo . "Get out of my sight! Get out of my house! Take this child away and never let me see her!" he yelled to anyone who could hear.

Ta Lo was so angry and so disappointed that he went into his chambers and wept bitterly. The jade box was later placed in the sanctuary with the household gods and never touched. The golden bell was not rung again for eighteen years, because it was eighteen years before the prophecies of the oracle were fulfilled.

No one knew what to do with this unwanted girl child.
Ta Lo had not said to drown her in the river, although
that was sometimes done in that period of the world's
history. But Ta Lo's older daughters, who knew what it
meant to be an unwanted girl child, felt sorry for this
infant and hurried forward from their hiding place to
take charge of her. As the oldest sister took the baby
in her arms and pulled back the blanket, they were
amazed at her beauty.

"What are we going to do with her?" asked the
middle sister.

"She will no doubt live with her mother," said the
third sister. "Her poor mother will be in disgrace because
she did not have a son."

"It is even more sad," said the first sister. "The nurse
told me that the child's mother died when she was born."

"Oh! Oh! Oh!" exclaimed the other two sisters.
"She is a sorry child."

"We need a happiness child in this household,"
said the third sister.

"We shall give her a happy name," said the first.

"It should be a singing name," said the second.

"It should have a surprise in it," said the third.

"We shall call her Si Ling Chi," said the first. The other two nodded. "It is a good name for a beautiful, unwanted girl child. Now we must take charge of her and see to it that our honorable disappointed father shall never see her."

But Ta Lo had already stormed out of his house, shouting, "I am not needed in this cursed household any longer. My Emperor needs me more and to him I will be as a father. Any problems you have, take to my old mother living in the hills. Only a woman is needed here and I have important duties to fulfill." He took only his most important belongings and departed for the royal palace.

Ta Lo wanted only to forget the whole unpleasant episode of the birth of Si Ling Chi as though it had never happened, but as soon as he arrived at his chambers in the royal palace, he came upon the young Emperor, who was waiting eagerly.

"Oh, you did get your wonderful son! I heard the golden bell ringing. Did you like my gift of the jade box?"

"Yes, Your Most Excellent Person, it was a beautiful gift."

"You may give it to your son when he is older. I want your wonderful son to have it."

"Dear child," said Ta Lo, "my wonderful son was not born. Another girl child was born. I do not wish to mention it again. I shall live the rest of my life here with you. You have no father, I have no son. We shall try to help each other."

"That will be a very good thing, Ta Lo. Perhaps I am glad that you had a girl child. Can you not bring her here to study with me sometimes?"

"No, I have no desire ever to see her."

"Of course," said Huang-Ti. "Then I shall never see her either. But, Ta Lo, if ever she wants the jade box, give it to her to console her for being a girl child." And this being said, the box was lost in the forgetfulness of dreams.

2

What Kind of Child Is This?

When Si Ling Chi was a few months old an important question arose. There was a very old custom in China, going back as far as any could remember. Girl children should have their feet bound. Dainty feet and small steps were considered necessary to be a fine lady. The three older sisters had had their feet bound and could only scamper about with mincing steps. "Shall we bind her feet?" the youngest sister asked. "A proper maid should have small feet."

"The child is enough trouble to us. I do not want to listen to her wails because her feet are bound," replied the second sister.

"No, we shall not be troubled by endless work for this child," said the older sister with authority. "She will not be seen at parties and balls any

20

more than we are. She will probably not even go to the
market place. She will certainly not go to the temple since
our father has built so large a shrine for the gods in his
house. He did this so that he would not have to display
his ugly daughters in the city. No, she will have no
need for fine styles or fashionable customs."

"You speak correctly," said the middle sister. "She will
never be seen beyond the house or garden."

The younger sister looked sadly at the laughing,
bright-eyed baby. "She is so beautiful," she whispered.
Aloud she said, "Ah, well, perhaps she will be happier
if she can run swiftly, like boys do. Boy children have
a happier time."

"Then we certainly will not bother ourselves or her
with binding," said the older sister. "We will do only
what is required of us, which is to look after her needs
and keep her out of sight of our father."

By the time she was a year old, Si Ling Chi was able
to move very fast on her not-bound feet. In fact, she was
hard to keep track of. "She fears nothing," exclaimed the
youngest sister one day when she was supposed to be
watching the baby. Si Ling Chi had wandered as far as
the stables without being seen. A servant had discovered

her standing close to the great black horse Thunder,
Ta Lo's finest stallion. Terrified, the man came running
to the three sisters, who were searching frantically for
the child.

"Come, come very quickly," he gasped. "Come and
get that small witch before she changes the Master's horse
into a devil or a dragon." The sisters could not run fast.

"Either we should bind her feet or grow wings on
ourselves," wheezed the middle sister, panting. She was
very fat and the unusual exertion made her puff.

"She should be beaten for such boldness," cried the
youngest sister.

"She shall be!" screamed the oldest, who was very tall
and thin and had fallen in her haste, but when they
arrived at the stable they were filled with astonishment.
Si Ling Chi stood patting the large beast, who only
turned his head to look at her, and when the child saw
her sisters she laughed and ran eagerly to them. The
oldest sister gathered her up in her arms. The second
reached out for her and then the third snatched her away,

but only to hug her in relief. They were glad to have found this strange, captivating baby unharmed.

With her feet not bound, Si Ling Chi moved faster and covered more ground than anyone in Ta Lo's household. She enjoyed going everywhere on the estate and wandering among the rocky hills above Ta Lo's grounds. She was at home in woods or fields.

"Perhaps we should have bound her feet for her safety if not for her elegance," said the youngest sister one day when they had been searching the whole afternoon for Si Ling Chi, who was now three years old.

"She may have been carried away by bears," said the second sister.

"Then let the bears have her," exclaimed the oldest who was no longer young enough to enjoy scrambling over rocky hills looking for a stupid girl child.

"Why do we disturb ourselves about this child?" asked the middle sister. "She is a witch and nothing will hurt her, but may the gods protect the rest of us!"

And so the years slipped by and Si Ling Chi grew in intelligence and beauty. She did seem to lead a charmed life, for she never had serious accidents. She was so joyous and carefree that her oldest sister thought she should be more quiet and sedate. It was not right or proper for a girl to grow up so undisciplined, and yet there was little for which the sisters could punish her.

"She isn't exactly a bad child," said the youngest sister when they were considering what further steps should be taken for her education. "She even proves herself very helpful around the house, but she seems to fear nothing and no one. It is very wrong to be so fearless."

"Perhaps we should take her more often to see the household gods. The gods always terrified me," said the middle sister.

"Yes, perhaps the gods would settle her down and make her more solemn," agreed the oldest.

"Perhaps," said the youngest sister, "but I am not sure that she will not upset the gods. She has a strange power over animals and other creatures. It almost seems as though she were on speaking terms with insects and snakes . . . ugh! She gives me the twitches all over!" The other sisters nodded their heads in agreement.

"But we shall try it," said the older. "We shall leave her there alone and perhaps that will sober her a bit. The household shrine is a dreary place and the great god Shoku-Po is very frightening."

"Be sure to tell her to sit before Shoku-Po and listen carefully to what he has to tell her," said the middle sister in a stern voice.

"Why do we not instruct the oracle to be there so that he can speak for the gods and put a little fright into her?" suggested the third sister.

"Oh, that is a very good plan," said the middle sister, who that morning had found a jar full of bugs and worms in the corner of the room where they all slept. She felt very strongly that Si Ling Chi should grow up fearing *something*.

The three sisters were well pleased with this conference and felt that the plan would suddenly make their little sister a more docile and quiet child. And their plan might have worked—had the oracle been in the shrine when they pushed Si Ling Chi through the door and closed it behind her.

If Si Ling Chi had been careful and timid like her three older sisters, she might have been frightened. She should have felt sober in the presence of the many stone figures that her family called the household gods. She had been given several tiny gods that she carried about like dolls. These she talked to and showed the many interesting things she found, but this was the first time in her life that she had ever been in the shrine where the larger household gods were kept. Some of these figures were made of jade, some were of marble, and others of amber. The great god Shoku-Po had a priceless pearl in his forehead.

He was the most important god of the people who were responsible to the Emperor. He upheld right actions, honesty, hard work, and responsibility. Si Ling Chi knew that he was the largest, most important god and that she was supposed to listen to him. It was for this god that the oracle was to have spoken, urging Si Ling Chi to be more obedient and careful, as was proper for a girl child to be. But the oracle had received a more urgent message to go to the palace just before Si Ling Chi entered the shrine.

Si Ling Chi sat before Shoku-Po for a long time listening. When she received no message she looked up shyly to see if perhaps he was angry with her. But there was a small smile on his stone lips and his deep eyes looked kindly.

"What would you have me do?" she asked. Perhaps it was she who should start the conversation. "I do not mean to be disobedient but there is so much of beauty and happiness in the world. There are such numbers of different creatures. There is so much to be danced, so much to be sung, and so many things to be touched, that only a happy little breeze could do it all. I would like to be a happy breeze, but I was made a girl so it is very hard to do."

Si Ling Chi had stood up to tell him all this and as she did so something astonishing happened. The great pearl in the god's forehead fell out. It fell right into Si Ling Chi's outstretched hands. She was so astonished that she was quiet for a long time. She stood peering at the great shimmering object in her hands. It had a thousand little lights. She thought it was the most beautiful thing that she had ever seen or touched. It seemed to whisper a little song as she touched it. She looked up at the god.

"Did you mean to have me look at it ?" she asked. "Are you letting me touch it as you would let a little breeze? Oh, thank you! Thank you!" she gasped. "I will be very careful not to lose it. May I hold it for a single day?" The god made no answer, but he didn't frown at her as she was sure he would if he was displeased. She was certain she had his permission, so she hurried out, clutching the great pearl joyously.

3

The Great Pearl Disappears

Si Ling Chi ran out into the garden to sit in her favorite place, under the great tree beside the wall around the Emperor's estates. A little fox came up to her, but he fled when she showed him the pearl. Then a white crow who made her nest in the great tree flew down to her. Si Ling Chi greeted it.

"You have not looked at me since the new moon arrived. Now you decide I am worth noticing since the great god Shoku-Po has let me take his pearl for a day. I can hold it for a whole day. See, I have it in my hand now."

Si Ling Chi held out the pearl for the bird to see. The crow snatched it in her beak and flew with it to her nest. Si Ling Chi ran after her, screaming, "Come back, sister crow!

Come back! You cannot have the pearl of the great god. You cannot! Come back!" But the crow sat blinking down at the frantic little girl.

Things could not have happened worse. Poco Shan soon returned from the palace and ran to the shrine of the household gods to see if he still had time to instruct Si Ling Chi. When the oracle discovered that the great pearl in the god's forehead was gone, he promptly fainted. When he came to, he thought he had had a bad dream. But when he saw the great gaping hole in the god's forehead, he grabbed his head and ran about, moaning. How could he tell Ta Lo? But he must tell him. He ran out of the shrine and sent a messenger to summon Ta Lo to come as quickly as possible.

"And what is this terrible crisis at my home that could not be taken care of by my mother?" demanded Ta Lo angrily.

"Something terrible has happened. Come!" cried Poco Shan. He led Ta Lo to the shrine and pointed to the largest god Shoku-Po. "The great pearl is gone. When I returned from the palace, I discovered it missing. It's gone . . . gone!"

"Thieves! Robbers! Villains!" screamed Ta Lo. "Don't stand there like a stupid donkey. We must find the pearl before Shoku-Po realizes his emblem of purity has been taken. Call the entire household. Call the servants. Call the guards. Find the culprit. Find out who was last in here. You are the oracle, though not a very good one, as I remember, but you had better be good now and find this pearl!"

The entire household and all the servants, even those from the stables, were summoned, since anyone on Ta Lo's estates might have entered the shrine. That is, everyone came except Si Ling Chi. No one remembered her in their terror and excitement. Besides, no grownup in his right mind would have thought it possible for this youngest daughter of Ta Lo, six years young and never seen very often in the house, to have known anything about the pearl. No one would have thought of her, that is, except her sisters, who knew she had been the last one in the dreary shrine, and her sisters did not underestimate Si Ling Chi. They looked carefully at each other now as Ta Lo demanded, "Who was the last person in here?"

Nobody answered his question.

"Would it have been Your Honorable Self?" questioned Poco Shan.

"Well, of course, I do pay my respects to our household gods so they will not think I have deserted my family," said Ta Lo. "Indeed, I hurried into the shrine last evening to consult Shoku-Po, but the pearl was there at that time. Who has been here today? Poco Shan, it is your duty to find the one and you shall be thrown into prison if you cannot. I have spoken. I give you until sunset to find the pearl."

The three sisters hurried out to find Si Ling Chi. They decided among themselves they would give her no chance to fib about it. If they acted as though they knew she had the pearl, she would be too frightened to deny it.

"Where is it, Si Ling Chi? Where have you put the pearl from the god's forehead? If you give it to us we will not beat you and we will not even tell our father, who is very angry about its being gone. You were the last one in the shrine so we know you have it," said the oldest sister in a very reasonable tone of voice.

"We know you have it," echoed the second.

"Give it to us this minute!" cried the third.

"I do not have it," said Si Ling Chi, "but I can tell you where it is."

"Where?" they all shouted.

"It is up there in the white bird's nest," said Si Ling Chi, pointing to the tree.

"How ridiculous," cried the oldest. "That is impossible. How could it get there?"

"How indeed?" repeated the second.

"How, how, how?" demanded the third.

"The white bird took it there," said Si Ling Chi, "because it was white like herself."

"Oh, why do we bother her about it?" said the oldest. "I do not believe such a story."

"How could so small a child know anything so important anyway?" said the second breathlessly.

"Quite impossible," agreed the third.

"But if you can produce that pearl you had better do it before sunset or poor Poco Shan will go to prison."

After her sisters had left her, Si Ling Chi sat hugging her knees. She didn't know what going to prison meant, but her sisters made it sound bad and Poco Shan could not know where the pearl was. She knew the oracle when she saw him. He always smiled at her as though she were somebody. She had never talked to any man except the stableboys, but she must tell this man called the oracle where the pearl was. Of course, it was high up in the tree and she didn't know how he would get it. That would be exciting to watch, though, so she would tell him.

Poco Shan was in the shrine, before the large god, kneeling with his head touching the floor and beating the floor with his hands in great distress.

"Show me where it is, speak to me in some small way so I can find the pearl."

Si Ling Chi stood just inside the shrine and watched. She crept forward slowly until she stood beside the oracle.

"Would you like me to tell you where the pearl is?" she whispered. Poco Shan was so startled he shot up like a jack-in-the-box.

"Oh, Si Ling Chi, how you scared me! How could you know where the pearl has disappeared?"

"I saw," she replied. "Come and I will show you." Poco Shan grabbed her by the hand and almost leaped out of the gloomy shrine.

"Where? Where is it?"

"I don't know how you can ever get it back," she said. "It is up there, high in that tree, in the white crow's nest."

Poco Shan grabbed his head and wailed, "Oh, no, no, no! It couldn't be!"

"It is unless she swallowed it, but I think it is too big for her throat, so she probably hid it in her nest. She likes bright, pretty things."

"How can you know? How could she ever get it from the god?"

"She didn't. She got it from me."

"And how did you get it?" demanded Poco Shan, grabbing her by the shoulders.

"My sisters put me in the shrine to listen to the household gods. None of them said anything to me." Suddenly Poco Shan remembered that he had been asked to talk to Si Ling Chi for Shoku-Po but had been detained.

"Yes, yes, and then what?"

"The god Shoku-Po dropped the great pearl into my hands when I was holding them out to him. He did not talk aloud but I know he told me I could keep the pearl for a whole day and feel its singing."

"Yes, yes, you felt its singing."

"Oh, yes, I felt its smooth white singing with the dawn sky in it. I showed it to my friend the little fox, but it made him sorry so he ran away. Then I showed the

white crow when she flew down to see what I had,
but she snatched it from my hand and flew right
up there to her nest."

"It is an unbelievable story so it could be true," muttered
Poco Shan, "and if it is true, what can we do then?"

"You could get the stableboy to climb up and look,"
said Si Ling Chi.

"Remember, Si Ling Chi, do not say what we are
looking for," said Poco Shan. "Then, if it is not in
the bird's nest we will not look foolish."

"I will say nothing," she answered. "Everyone thinks
I can know nothing important, that I am only a foolish
child, and that you would lose face if you were to listen
to me. I am such a poor thing, my honorable father,
Ta Lo, never talks to me or even looks at me."

Poco Shan was a kind man and now he felt sorry for
Ta Lo's youngest daughter. Then he remembered that it
had been indicated on the night she was born that she
was destined to do something very important in her life.
Maybe this was it. Or perhaps this was the beginning.
He was so excited that he ran to the stables himself to
find a boy and a rope to help the boy climb. When
Poco Shan returned with the stableboy to the tree under

which Si Ling Chi sat waiting, he said to the boy,
"I want you to bring me that bird's nest."

The stableboy jumped back. "Poco Shan, that is a bad
omen. We think the white bird brings bad luck. We all
call her White Bird of Sorrow."

"You will have no bad luck," said Poco Shan. "Ta Lo,
the Master, wishes you to bring him the bird's nest."

"I will help you go up the tree, Poco Shan, but the
white color of the bird means death and sorrow,"
cried the boy.

"I would get it if I could climb so high," offered
Si Ling Chi. "Just being born, my sisters say, was bad
luck for me, and the white bird is my friend."

"I have a good thought!" cried the stableboy. "In the
stable is a basket. Put her into it. I will get on the lower
branch and pull her into the tree. We will pull her up
in the basket. I will throw the rope higher and higher
over branches and pull her up and up until she can
reach the nest."

"Oh, that would be good," cried Si Ling Chi. "I will
just look in the nest and take what we are looking for
and not disturb the bird's home."

As the basket was brought and the strong banana-shoots

rope thrown over a limb to make it possible for the
stableboy to climb into the tree, a large crowd of servants
and their families gathered to watch Si Ling Chi hoisted
from one branch to another. There were shouts and cheers
when she reached the nest. She stood up and looked in.
Among the pieces of shell and sparkling beads was the
huge pearl, which Si Ling Chi took and held tightly
in her hand.

When she was brought down, everyone crowded
around her to exclaim over her daring and bravery.
Poco Shan took the pearl from her and ran to the shrine
to put it back before anything else could happen to it.
He reported to Ta Lo that he had found the pearl and
had securely fastened it in place. Ta Lo was so overjoyed
with the outcome of the event, he did not think to ask
where the pearl had been and so returned to the palace.

4

巳

Omen
of the
White Crow

When Si Ling Chi's sisters heard the shouting, they hurried out. "What has happened?" demanded the oldest.

"Si Ling Chi found the pearl Poco Shan was looking for," cried several servants looking amazed. "Is she not a wonderful child? She must be some kind of magic maker. How could the pearl get into the bird's nest and how could the child know? And she had no fear to get it from the white bird."

"Truly, she is no natural child," said another.

"I think she is a genie," cried another. "She is no ordinary common child."

"Listen to that!" whistled the second.

"She's a little devil, all right," muttered the third.

"Come, Si Ling Chi," said her older sister, reaching for her. Later she told the other two, "It will be very bad if our father hears of this; he has little patience or belief in genii and even less in children who make magic. Let us consult Poco Shan and see what we should do."

They ran to find Poco Shan. He told them that he had replaced the pearl and that Ta Lo had left for the palace without knowing who had taken the pearl. He suggested that it might be best if Si Ling Chi were taken away from the house for a while so the servants would calm down and stop talking about her magic.

"Yes, our little sister should disappear for a while," agreed the oldest sister.

"That is a good idea," chimed the second.

"Where shall we have her disappear?" asked the third.

"We shall take her to our grandmother's house and hide her for a year," said the first. "Grandmother lives in a little house a long way from here and she will put up with no nonsense from our little sister."

"She is a fierce old woman," said the second.

"I always thought she was an evil spirit," shuddered the third. "Yes, she will make that wild youngster quiet down and forget to be a genie."

After everyone had gone away and Si Ling Chi was bathed and looking very sweet and demure, the three sisters took her aside to talk to her.

"Si Ling Chi, little sister, we want to know what really happened today. We think that only you in the entire household would dare to touch the god Shoku-Po. It was you who took the pearl.

"That was a dreadful thing to do. Ta Lo was very angry. You are a very disobedient child and other people get punished for your sins. Poco Shan was almost exiled in disgrace because the pearl was gone.

"Our father Ta Lo was very angry and nobody dares tell him you took the pearl or he might feed all of us to the snow panther."

"Why?" asked Si Ling Chi.

"Because we are worthless girls," cried the third.

"Why are girls worthless?" asked the child. "Why would he give us to the snow panther to eat?"

"Sometimes if a man has too many girls that is what he does, but our father Ta Lo is a good father and I do not think he will do that," said the oldest. "But now he is angry and we are going to take you to live with our father's mother, who lives up in the hills. She is very old and very wise. She will teach you many things and everyone will forget about you."

"It will be a hard life, Si Ling Chi," wheezed her second sister. "She's almost as bad as the snow panther."

"You had better be obedient with her or she may do another thing they do to miserable girls. She may drown you in the river," declared the third sister.

"We go tomorrow," said the oldest. "It is a long journey by donkey, so we will leave early."

Si Ling Chi was given a bowl of rice, and then her three sisters left her alone. She didn't feel much like eating, so she put the bowl aside and lay down on her mat to cry. She had not often cried in her life because all life seemed so good and she was usually very happy. If she were not so frightened she would have been very glad to ride a donkey up in the mountains to see her honorable grandmother, but now she was afraid of what would happen to her. She cried very quietly. But her last thought before falling asleep was that she was going to ride a donkey. Nothing was ever all sad for Si Ling Chi.

So, Si Ling Chi was taken to her grandmother's house. The grandmother was an ancient person. She was her father's mother and managed Ta Lo's household with an

iron hand, seeing that the great feasts were correctly served and the food expertly cooked. She saw to it that there was little idleness among the slaves and servants. She was equally watchful that the children on the estate were properly fed. Even the domestic animals were well treated under her supervision. She was a wrinkled, gnarled woman, reportedly nearly a hundred years old. She seldom stirred from her sedan chair but was carried on the shoulders of two young men to the farthest reaches of Ta Lo's estates. She saw to it, too, that there was no waste.

Grandmother lived in a little house on a hill. A path

of flat stones wound up to the house, which was set in a grove of oleander trees. Here, with three servants, the old lady lived, and here the three older daughters of Ta Lo brought their young, mischievous sister.

"Most honorable and reverend grandmother," said the oldest sister, bowing low, "it has been brought to our attention that this little sister is growing very bold and disobedient. We wish to hide her for fear our honorable father's displeasure might cause him to sell us into slavery."

"What terrible thing has this young one done?" demanded the old woman.

All three of the older girls buried their faces in their arms, filled with fear and shame. But Si Ling Chi, stepping forward and bowing low, addressed her grandmother.

"I will tell you," she said clearly. "It was I who took the beautiful pearl that was in the head of the household god Shoku-Po. He gave it to me to hold for a single day. The white bird took it from me and hid it in her nest, but I was pulled up in a basket and got it with the stableboy's help. Poco Shan returned it to Shoku-Po."

At this confession the older sisters wailed, "Oh, woe! Woe! Woe!" and jumped back.

"Our father does not know who took it. We consider it wiser for our own sakes not to tell him that it was Si Ling Chi," said the middle sister.

"Leave her with me," snapped the old woman. "I will keep her and try to make her respectful."

The sisters scampered away like frightened hares, and Si Ling Chi stayed to live with her grandmother.

The one year that she was to have been hidden stretched into seven. She never forgot those years. She learned to weave, making coarse mats from tough fragrant grasses. She learned to spin thread from flax and to make bright dyes from plants and clays. She found time and opportunity to make friends with the insects and animals of the hills and fields around her grandmother's home. She learned to love her severe old grandmother as she had loved no one before. She didn't look forward to returning home.

5

五

The Jade and Sandlewood Box

Toward the end of the seventh year, the old grandmother died and Si Ling Chi returned to her father's house. She was now twelve years old.

One day when her sisters had gone away and her father was absent from home, Si Ling Chi entered the family shrine to see her old friend Shoku-Po, who had permitted her to take the pearl. It was then that for the first time she noticed the jade and sandlewood box, the gift from the Emperor to the wonderful son Ta Lo never had. It was very beautiful and after stepping back she took it and addressed Shoku-Po:

"Since you permitted me to take your great pearl for a single day, would you let me take this beautiful jade box?" It seemed to her that the god gave a smiling consent, so she

48

hid the beautiful box under her tunic and scurried out. She ran to the great tree to examine the box more closely.

"It is like a little palace," murmured Si Ling Chi when she saw the birds and trees and flowers of gold carved around the many hidden compartments. "My little yellow snake would live like an emperor in this jade box." She ran to get the yellow snake from the mat of grasses where she kept him in the sunny corner of the courtyard.

"There is also room for little brother lizard," she said, hurrying to take the green lizard from a stone jar in the garden. Then she found a leafy twig with a woolly, black caterpillar on it. She laid the twig and caterpillar in another section of the box.

"Be happy, little brothers," she crooned. "Live together in peace. Have I not given you a beautiful palace in which to live?"

At this time Ta Lo was very busy with affairs pertaining to the empire, for it was his responsibility to find a suitable bride for the Emperor Huang-Ti, who was now nearly eighteen years old. It was time he had a wife, an Empress of China. Ta Lo had been away from home for many cycles of the moon when finally, in the summer, he returned home and discovered that his jade box was missing. He was very angry and threatened the family and servants with punishment if the box was not found. The three older daughters held a brief conference and set out to find their youngest sister.

Si Ling Chi had built a small stone fortress by the lily pond, where she kept the jade box hidden. Here every day she permitted her pets to eat and enjoy the sun, while she cleaned and polished the box. As they died from time to time or escaped, she would replace them with new specimens from the hills and fields. On this day, she had finished putting the yellow snake, the green lizard, and her other pets into the box when she saw her three sisters approaching. She pulled up her knees, covered with bright red trousers, beneath her chin, and waited for them.

The oldest of the three began, "Little sister, we have come to speak with you concerning a matter of much importance. You know that our father is very great and very honorable. He is High Counselor to the Emperor."

"Yes, indeed," said the second sister. "We are a very noble family, known throughout the whole kingdom of China."

"But we are also a miserable family because we have no sons," said the third sister. "Four times our father has been married and each time a girl child has been born. That is a great misfortune for any family."

"A dreadful misfortune!" said the oldest sister.

"Woe! Woe! Woe!" said the other two, rocking back and forth.

"What is a worse fate for our father," said the third sister, "the three of us are ugly and he cannot arrange marriages for us, but you, little sister, are very beautiful to look at. If you were only good, our father might arrange a fine marriage for you."

"But you are full of wickedness. You are a disgrace to our family," stated the second sister.

"Go bring us the jade box at once, or we shall be tempted to beat you!" hissed the third sister, very red in the face.

"If I were to give you the beautiful green sandlewood box," said Si Ling Chi, "would I then see my honorable father?"

"May the gods have mercy on her!" shouted the first sister.

"He would probably like to get his hands on the person who stole it," choked the second sister.

"We should take her to him," said the third.

"Why do I never see my father?" demanded Si Ling Chi.

"Our father does not want to look at another girl," said the oldest, looking very sad. The other two exclaimed, "Woe! Woe! Woe!" and ran around in a little circle. Suddenly they jumped at Si Ling Chi and the youngest sister caught her by the neck of her tunic and yanked her to her feet. They looked very threatening. For once she was really frightened of them. They had never been quite so angry before. But she would not let them see that she was frightened. She cocked her head on one side and said, "Why do you accuse me of taking the jade box?"

"It was you who took the pearl from the household god when you were younger," answered the first sister, "so we are certain you have taken the jade box, and our father is very angry that it is gone. Go get it for us this minute before we are all disowned!"

"Don't you know that we are four worthless girls in the eyes of our father?" choked the second sister.

At this speech Si Ling Chi wrenched free of her sister's grasp and stamped her foot. "I am not worthless!" she exclaimed. "I will show my father that I am not worthless. I will be like a son and bring him honor someday."

"In the meantime, bring us that jade box!" hissed the third sister.

Si Ling Chi ran to her hiding place and brought out the jade box, her sisters following her.

"Oh, joy! Joy! Joy!" exclaimed the oldest sister. "It is found at last. Now we shall not be beaten!"

"We always suffer for your wickedness," cried the second, whistling like an exploding firecracker.

"You are a terrible, terrible child!" shrieked the third. "Give us that box before we beat you here and now."

They reached out three pairs of hands to snatch it from her, but Si Ling Chi held it high above her head and said, "First let me take out my little pets. There are many and you might forget to feed them properly."

"Pets!" screeched the sisters, and they jumped back.

"You have something alive in there?" demanded the first.

"Is it really alive?" wheezed the second.

"Is it one of your crawling creatures?" screamed the third.

Si Ling Chi peeped into the jade box, smiling impishly, "I have only four at present," she answered. "I have a beautiful bronze beetle—a big one!" The sisters all jumped back. "A grasshopper with big jaws who sometimes spits at me. There is a green and gorgeous lizard; and the best of all because it was so hard to catch, a yellow snake!"

Si Ling Chi's sisters fled to a safe distance behind a weeping willow tree. Another figure came up behind her as she laughed and said, "Oh, those three silly sisters of mine."

This person was Ta Lo himself. Si Ling Chi did not see or hear him approach, but her sisters did and were fascinated to see what would happen now.

"Just why have you taken my jade box, my gift from the Emperor, for your pets?" he demanded angrily.

Si Ling Chi whirled about and faced her father for the first time in her life. For once she was speechless. She backed up slowly as he advanced menacingly. Watching at a distance, the first sister wrung her hands in despair. The second wheezed in consternation, while the third nearly fainted and clung to the other two for support. They really loved their exasperating younger sister and had dedicated their lives to protecting her from Ta Lo. Now, it seemed, she would at last be caught in the very act of offending him and they would probably witness her destruction. This they could not bear! They would never understand her, but they admired both her beauty and courage. What could they do now?

"You—you are Ta Lo?" stammered Si Ling Chi. "You are my honorable father?"

"I am Ta Lo. I suppose you are that wretched daughter I have never seen."

Si Ling Chi bowed very low and said, "I, most honorable father, am Si Ling Chi, a most miserable girl. I regret that I am not a son."

"But you have been so audacious as to take my jade box, a gift from the Emperor."

She bowed very low and said, "It was I who took it. And it was I who took the pearl from Shoku-Po many years ago."

Her straightforwardness startled Ta Lo, who was accustomed to creating confusion and humility in those he rebuked. He said, "In some ways you have the boldness of a son. But why have you taken the jade box?"

"It was serving no useful purpose," answered Si Ling Chi promptly. "To be truly beautiful things should also be useful. Is that not so, my father?" She looked at him inquiringly. "All China is making useful and beautiful materials and tools because you have said that was true. The jade box sat on the shelf looking useless and idle. My little pets needed a house."

"What are your pets?" asked Ta Lo.

Si Ling Chi ran to him eagerly. "These are my little brothers of the brown earth. These are my little sisters of the green fields, and I love them. See, isn't that a beautiful brown beetle? And here is a gorgeous green lizard, a little yellow snake. . . ."

"May the gods protect us!" shouted Ta Lo. "You may look like a daughter but you are more like a son."

"Honorable Father, someday I will bring you the honor a son would have brought you."

At this speech Ta Lo laughed heartily. "Ho! Ho! Ho! The honor of a son! Your thoughts as well as your actions are bold. That could never be." Ta Lo started to leave, then turned. "But tell me, how do you propose to bring me honor?"

"Perhaps you could arrange a marriage for me to someone of importance," suggested Si Ling Chi.

"Heaven help us!" exclaimed Ta Lo, stepping back in astonishment. "It will be well to marry you to someone even if he isn't important!" Ta Lo hurried away and Si Ling Chi held the jade box.

"Wait, most honorable father," she called. "You do not have your jade box. I will free my pets."

Ta Lo, who had always taken an interest in the wild
life of hills and fields, now turned to answer and said,
"Since you have a love for creatures of the outdoors,
a love such as I have always had, I will try to get for you
a curious white moth with black lines upon its wings.
I have never seen it except in the Emperor's garden.
There are mulberry trees in his garden, and this moth
feeds on the leaves of this tree. Perhaps I can get some
of these moths for you."

"Oh, thank you, honorable father. Your humble and
undeserving daughter is grateful," said Si Ling Chi.

"You may keep the jade box," said Ta Lo. "Perhaps
it really belongs to you after all, even though you are
not a son." Then he hurried away.

The three sisters watching from behind the willow
tree were amazed.

"She has bewitched our father," exclaimed the first.

"He listened to her idle words and did not beat her,"
said the second.

"He gave her the jade box, his gift from the Emperor!"
said the third.

But Si Ling Chi was much too excited and happy
to notice them.

6 六
In the Emperor's Garden

The seasons passed with their accustomed rhythm of changing colors—the frosty starkness of barren trees, the fresh green filled with the warmth and brightness of spring. Si Ling Chi was most obedient, doing the household tasks appointed to her, and she did not see her father again for a long time.

Affairs of state demanded much time from Ta Lo as the most difficult task of his long career with the young Emperor continued to worry him. Although Huang-Ti's father had married many times after Ta Lo became Chief Counselor, it had never been difficult to find him a wife. But now he had the responsibility of finding a first wife for the son. There were many suitable maidens from among eligible families, but the young

59

man insisted on seeing his bride before he married her.
This was not according to the rules of proper society, but
the Emperor was a stubborn young man. Ta Lo traveled
far and wide searching for a suitable bride who would be
willing to permit the young Emperor to see her before
asking for her hand. This was indeed an embarrassing
problem for Ta Lo and he grew quite thin and morose
trying to do his duty.

For once in their lives since Si Ling Chi had been born
her sisters were living easily and comfortably. Now that
Ta Lo had at last seen and accepted his youngest daughter
and not disowned her and them, they could relax.

A year passed and Si Ling Chi's father failed to keep
his promise to bring her a beautiful moth from the
Emperor's garden. Therefore, when the cherry trees were
in bloom again and the beetles were sunning themselves
on the garden wall, Si Ling Chi made a resolution. She
would go to the garden of the Emperor herself and find
the white moth with black-striped wings her father had
told her about.

This was not an easy thing for her to accomplish.
She gave it much thought. First, she must get some boy's
clothing. Her home was so completely one of women that

boy's clothes were never seen except on the gardeners or the few menservants. Si Ling Chi dared not give herself away by asking them for their trousers or coats.

"I do believe that our little sister will grow into a quite respectable woman, after all," said the oldest sister to the other two. She had been watching Si Ling Chi, who had been sitting quietly an entire morning, trying to figure a way to get boy's clothing.

"Perhaps," answered the middle sister, "but I think we should be very cautious yet another season."

"I think we should be preparing for some new disaster from her," said the youngest sister. "She has been too good for too long and this studied silence probably means that she is thinking up something that may cost all of us our heads."

"I think she has improved since we bought her the two beautiful robes," said the first sister. "Now that she has outgrown trousers and tunics, she has grown into the likeness of a young lady."

"And putting her hair up has helped," said the youngest sister. "She is very beautiful."

"I shall wait another season to believe that she has really become a lady," said the middle sister.

"She's just too good."

If they could have seen Si Ling Chi at that moment they would have agreed with this sister. Si Ling Chi was borrowing her middle sister's red trousers. These pants were a source of embarrassment to her sister because they were so very big. She was quite fat and they were very comfortable to relax in. She wore them only in the privacy of their sleeping room and kept them in her chest, well covered with other clothing. Si Ling Chi's own trousers, that she had worn when younger, showed wear so badly that when she was given young ladies' attire, her sisters had thrown them away.

Now she must get a boy's shirt or a tunic. This was not too difficult, for on a hot day the gardener hung his on a bush. He threatened to beat all of the young gardeners when it disappeared, but this did not bring it back. From then on all the gardeners avoided the spot because they believed that a devil had taken possession of that part of the garden.

Her hair was not too great a problem. She piled it on her head and put a wide-brimmed hat over it. She took a basket from the kitchen, filled it with peaches, and tied a long vine to it.

Since Ta Lo's house was situated next to the palace grounds and was separated from it by only a high wall, Si Ling Chi decided to climb the willow tree that grew higher than the wall. It was not as big around the trunk as the elm tree in which the white crow had had its nest when Si Ling Chi was younger, so she could climb it by herself. She put the jade box into her fruit basket so that she would have a place to keep any white moths she might catch. She hid the basket beneath the willow tree in readiness for the next day's venture.

The next day when the Emperor was in his garden, he was amazed to hear, "Stop, boy!" A gardener was waving a sickle and chasing a slim figure in boy's clothes. "This is the Emperor's garden, a sacred place, and you cannot enter."

"But I have a gift for the Emperor. I wish to give him a basket of fruit."

The person the gardener was chasing was Si Ling Chi dressed in her sister's red trousers, the gardener's coat, and a wide-brimmed hat. She had climbed the tree in her father's yard, then let down her basket of fruit by the long vine when no one was around, just as she had planned it. She had then climbed onto the wall

surrounding the Emperor's garden and waited. When
no one could be seen she had lowered herself and
dropped to the ground.

After picking up her basket, she had cautiously made
her way to the lake where the swans were sunning
themselves. Suddenly, a white moth flew by. She dropped
the basket, grabbed the jade box, and ran after it. At that
moment the gardener, who was cutting the long grass by
the lake, saw her. Brandishing his sickle, he chased her,
shouting, "Stop boy! Stop, I say!"

When he finally caught her, he shook her roughly,
saying, "Do you not know this is the Emperor's garden?
It is a holy place. You cannot enter here."

"But I am here. I have brought a basket of fruit for
the Emperor. See, it is over there by the tall yew tree."

"But that is not the proper thing to do," cried the
gardener. "The proper way to give a gift to the Emperor
is to send it with a messenger, who will deliver it at
the garden gate."

"I wanted to bring the gift myself. It was said by a
wise man that a humble gift is worth more when it is
presented with a smiling face by the giver."

"But no one presents a gift directly to the Emperor."

"But I think he would like to receive a gift directly from one who loves him and wishes to give him a gift."

The gardener was becoming more angry and Si Ling Chi should have been frightened, but she was becoming amused at his irritation as she was amused when her sisters were angry with her. She regarded him impudently.

"How did you get in here?" he demanded. "The royal walls are too high to climb. Soldiers guard every entrance, yet I turn around from my work and find you running around grabbing at the air. Perhaps you are a devil. Tell me now, how did you get in?"

"I *am* a devil," answered the girl. "I will tell you a secret. I have always been here. I grew in a cabbage head and every time I see you coming I hide. But I have always lived in the Emperor's garden."

The little man jumped up and down in a rage. "If you were not so young and if I did not want to make an unclean spot in the Emperor's garden, I would cut off your head now!" he shouted, waving his sickle wildly.

Just at this moment one of the white moths flew by and Si Ling Chi sprang after it. The gardener might have pursued her farther had not the Emperor appeared from around a large bush. From where he had been reclining

he had seen and heard the gardener and Si Ling Chi,
but she had not seen him nor did she see him motion
for the angry gardener to leave.

Si Ling Chi was still trying to keep an eye on the moth
she wanted to capture. "I almost had you, little brother,"
she cried, dashing behind a tree as the gardener
disappeared. "Perhaps I will be beaten for all my pains
to come here, perhaps I will be thrown into a dungeon
by the Emperor, who is a hard man. I have never seen
him but my sisters have told me that he is very ugly.
I will not mind if I can just capture you and several
of your brothers and sisters."

Suddenly, Huang-Ti ran forward and caught the moth
for her. "Here is one," he said. "Look, there is another."
Si Ling Chi ran and caught the second one. "I have
two more," cried this new friend, "but where are
you keeping them?"

"In here," said Si Ling Chi, and she pulled the jade box
from inside her tunic. The Emperor put the moths into

the jade box and then studied it very hard. Where had
he seen this box? He was sure that he had seen it
somewhere, sometime. It was the jade box he had seen
in his childhood dreams so often, in which he thought
his future was locked. Could it be real now?

"What do you want these moths for and who are you?"
he asked, handing the jade box to Si Ling Chi.

Si Ling Chi became very confused. "Oh, Sir, I am just
a worthless boy." She had noted the fine linen robe with
the golden neckband and all her confidence left her.
Who this person was she did not know, but he must surely
be someone close to the Emperor and very important.
Perhaps, he might even be someone who knew her father.
"I thank you for helping me catch the moths and now I
will leave." She bowed low and backed away, clutching
the jade box.

"Wait, not so fast," said Huang-Ti. "It is my duty to
know who you are and how you happened to be in
the royal garden."

"But Your Honor, I have told you that I am a worthless
boy who has brought a basket of peaches to the Emperor."

"But to be a boy is not so worthless, especially a boy
smart enough to get into the Emperor's garden when it

is so well guarded," answered this stranger. "Besides, only girls are considered worthless."

This speech made Si Ling Chi more embarrassed still. "I mean, Your Honor, that I am a worthless boy only when I am found in the Emperor's garden. I hope that you will not tell him that such a one was found in his garden." She backed away and Huang-Ti followed.

"Are you quite sure you are a boy, even an unworthy boy?" he asked, enjoying her increasing embarrassment.

"Yes, yes," she stammered. "I am indeed a very excellent boy, a very worthy son."

"I doubt that very much," said Huang-Ti. "For one thing, you are much too beautiful to be really a worthless son. You have mincing ways like a foolish girl."

This speech almost threw Si Ling Chi into a panic. She backed away, bobbing her head up and down. "If you will pardon this most unworthy boy, I will take my basket of fruit to the Emperor's cook and depart."

But the young Emperor was more than interested in this strange girl in this motley assortment of boy's clothing. "Why do you come here and who are you?" he demanded. "What do you wish to do with the white moths that live in the Emperor's garden?"

"I will keep them in the jade box, the palace of all my creatures," she explained.. "See, there are many compartments. I have many pets. I have a bronze beetle. In here is a green lizard. And here is my little brother snake." She held the snake up for him to see. After she had finished showing him her creatures, the Emperor caught her hand and took the jade box from her.

"I *have* seen this box before. Where did you get it? It is no ordinary box. Where did you get it?"

Si Ling Chi had never fainted in her life but her head was truly whirling at this question. "I—I—Oh, please Sir, I must go quickly." She would have fled had the Emperor not held her by the arm.

"To what family do you belong?" he asked.

"I am only a stupid servant boy. I come from the country."

"We shall see," said the Emperor. "I shall take you to Ta Lo, the Emperor's High Counselor, and see if he knows who you are. I shall keep the jade box to help me find out who you are." The Emperor started for the royal palace, pulling Si Ling Chi after him. But with a sudden burst of energy, she wrenched herself free, grabbed the jade box, and fled to the high hedge along the wall.

七

Richi-Po the Matchmaker Has an Adventure

Si Ling Chi had so swiftly dodged in and out among the shrubs and bushes of the Emperor's garden, dropping to the ground when she might have been seen, that Huang-Ti lost her and didn't see her scramble up the tree and over the wall several hours later, when she felt it was safe to return the way she had come.

This had been the most fascinating thing that had ever happened to the young Emperor. He was old enough now to know that there were no devils, genii, spirits, or enchanted creatures, such as one's governesses told stories about. Besides Ta Lo, his constant teacher, did not believe much in such creatures; but he could not figure out how this strange maid, dressed in red trousers, could have gotten into his garden. The gardener

71

had checked all the gates. They were all locked and barred. And the garden was enclosed by a very high wall. She could hardly be real. But he hadn't been dreaming. Was Ta Lo trying some kind of magic on him to make him want a wife? He was getting more insistent all the time that the Emperor start proceedings to obtain a wife. Huang-Ti hated to ask him about this strange affair because he didn't want to get on the subject of matrimony again.

Then there was the matter of the jade and sandlewood box. There was something so familiar about it. Surely he had seen it somewhere, but where? Huang-Ti was so troubled that he could scarcely think of anything else, but he would not tell Ta Lo about it.

He remembered having seen a box like it in the royal palace somewhere. He searched among the mementos of his ancestors. He spent hours looking through parchment scrolls in the great library of the palace but nowhere was there even a picture of such a box.

And the contents of the box—the lizard, the bronze beetle, and one yellow snake! Were these strange symbols? "I must find her! I must find her!" he screamed to his own silent chambers and beat his head with his fists.

Ta Lo had once succeeded in getting the young Emperor to a matchmaker, whose business it was to make suitable marriages between families whose children were ready to marry. A matchmaker arranged the interviews between parents of the bride and groom and helped negotiate suitable dowries. Marriage was never arranged by the young people who were being married, and the groom never saw his bride until after the marriage ceremony when he first removed the veil that concealed her face.

Suddenly Huang-Ti had an inspiration, but he would not tell Ta Lo. He was sure that Ta Lo would never approve of his plan. Of course, he did not need Ta Lo's approval. He could do whatever he wanted. He was Emperor and need not take orders from anyone, but he was always finding out that there was an invisible authority stronger than any other that made some things right or wrong without anybody telling you. But he had to find this strange girl. At least he had to find out if she had been real or if he had dreamed her. He had to know or he would go out of his mind thinking about it.

He now had a plan to find her, but he would not tell Ta Lo about it, for Ta Lo was always so correct and proper, he would surely not approve. He would have to tell someone, though. That someone would have to be a matchmaker, for only one of legal standing could even approach the fathers of eligible daughters. He sent for Richi-Po, the matchmaker he and Ta Lo had once consulted, and advised him in the message not to say anything of this visit to Ta Lo.

"I am about to search for a bride, Richi-Po, but I need your help. I have seen the lady of my choice. She is young, not quite a lady, and I am not certain where to find her. The one way you will be sure to know her is by the jade box she carries, which contains several live insects and a yellow snake. These she calls her little brothers. The jade box is a mystery to me since I seem to have seen it sometime but I can't remember where or when. Here is one I have made to resemble it. Put a lizard, a beetle, a yellow snake, and several white moths with black markings in it. Then show the box and its contents to all the maids you interview," directed Huang-Ti to the astonished matchmaker.

"But how can I arrange for you to know if this young-not-quite-a-lady is the proper woman to become Empress of China?"

"I have met this young lady in my own garden, but I
don't know whether she was real or a dream. It is
unbelievable that she was real, but I cannot quite
persuade myself that she was a dream. I need your help."

Richi-Po stared at the Emperor in astonishment. The
Emperor sometimes traveled outside the palace walls,
heavily guarded. He had vast estates where he rode
horseback. He was now old enough to go with Ta Lo
on important matters of state, but Richi-Po could think of
no time when he could have met an unchaperoned young
lady, and properly chaperoned young ladies did not look
at young men, much less talk to them. Anyway, no young
lady ever had the opportunity to look at or speak to the
Emperor. "This is a most improper way for any man to
select a bride! I am shocked at Your Highness!"
cried Richi-Po.

"Oh, but unusual methods are required to find her,
Richi-Po. She has great beauty. She is not a coward.
I believe that all China will be pleased with my choice,
if we can only find her. Report to me if you discover such
a maid. And do not say anything to Ta Lo about this.
He would not approve."

Huang-Ti had never seen anyone so shocked as the

matchmaker. "All of this is highly improper. It is not right for a young man to see his young bride."

"On the contrary," said the Emperor. "It is only reasonable that a man see the woman he is going to choose to be his wife."

"But that is not the custom," cried Richi-Po and turned to leave.

"I do not care what the custom is!" the Emperor shouted. "I shall hunt and hunt until I find this woman of my choice, and, Richi-Po, I command you to undertake this mission for me."

Richi-Po had arranged many marriages, but the request the Emperor was making for his marriage was strangest of all. He could not help wondering if the determined young man had taken leave of his senses. He considered what the Emperor wanted to be in very poor taste. But Huang-Ti was no ordinary mortal. He was loved beyond any other Emperor and was regarded as a god. Richi-Po now considered it a life and death matter to carry out this assignment.

"But this is so improper! This is such an impossible duty! This could get my head chopped off!"

"You may need to travel to the farthest regions of the

Empire, or you may find the maid of my choice within
the walls of the city. When you do find a maid, a beautiful
maid, who will recognize this box, and who will not run
when you show her the yellow snake, and who will
shout with joy at the white moths, find her father
and make the necessary arrangements for a joyous
and astonishing wedding. This is the maid I want
to be the Empress of China."

After his conference with the Emperor, Richi-Po felt
so doubtful of the mission on which he was being sent,
he was tempted to run away. He did not believe that
many maidens of China's royal families would submit
pleasantly to the test that Huang-Ti wished him to put
to them. But he mounted a white horse and set out for
the northern province of Gunga Dipan. The prince of this
province had an eligible daughter and he received the
matchmaker with enthusiasm and much honor.

"I am Richi-Po, the matchmaker, sent here by the
Emperor," he began. "His Highness understands that
you have a marriageable daughter."

"Oh yes! Oh yes and indeed!" exclaimed the fat prince,
squinting through his crafty eyes. "The Emperor will
make a wise decision if he chooses my daughter Lotus

Blossom for his wife. Yes and indeed, I soon shall arrange this happy event!"

"Not so fast," said Richi-Po. "The Emperor insists on certain qualities in a bride before he makes a settlement. He wants a young bride."

"My daughter is very young and I have fine horses to keep His Highness supplied if he marries my Lotus Blossom. After all, a woman is a woman."

"Not to the Emperor, who is still young and a dreamer," replied Richi-Po. "However, he seems to require courage in his bride, even above beauty. I am to conduct a small, harmless test to see if the lady is courageous. May I see Lotus Blossom and conduct my small test?"

"Indeed and indeed!" cried the excited Prince. He called for his servants and sent for Lotus Blossom, his only daughter. But Richi-Po's heart fell when the Princess stood before him, fat like her father and very young. Surely, this overfed child would not be a proper Empress. However, he would dutifully fulfill all the requirements. He took the jade box from his traveling bag and held it before the stupid-looking girl.

"This will in no way harm you," said the matchmaker. "I will open this box and show you a small surprise which

the Emperor wishes his bride to look upon." The girl
stood watching with her mouth open, as the matchmaker
cautiously opened the compartment containing the yellow
snake. He himself did not like this snake business though

he knew the snake to be harmless. The little snake poked out his head and flicked his tongue.

"Eeeeek!" screamed Lotus Blossom as she collapsed in a soft heap.

"Help!" screamed the Prince. "I have been deceived! You are no matchmaker from the Emperor. If you are, the Emperor of China is a monster, son of a she-dragon. I think you are an imposter. I shall have you thrown into a den of serpents!"

But Richi-Po did not wait one second to make his escape. While the Prince, with his eyes closed, screamed for help, dancing around his daughter, the matchmaker slipped through a narrow panel into a secret chamber. This opened onto a tiny indoor garden from where he could hear the servants running in response to the summons of the Prince. Richi-Po dodged in and out of rooms until he reached the kitchens. Here the servants were unaware of the turmoil in the other part of the house, but no stranger was ever permitted in the royal kitchens, as a protection against poisoning the Prince. A huge cook holding a very large butcher knife stood beside the door.

The matchmaker would escape with his life from this
venture only if he were brave. He pushed into the
kitchen, smiling cheerfully. "Good day and happy
cooking!" he greeted. "I am a traveling cook from the
kitchen of the Emperor. I bring a load of new sweets for
your Prince and wish to check on your spices that they
may be served properly."

"A cook from the Emperor's kitchen!" gasped the
servants. "He is someone of great importance. You can
tell by the fine golden band around his neck.
You can tell by his fine trousers and tunic."

But Richi-Po dared not waste precious time. "I will
see to my load in the court," he cried. "Prepare to show
me your best spices." He hurried through the bamboo
curtains covering the back doorway. He had not run for
years. His dignity made it difficult now, but he found his
legs moving very fast. The amazed servants, watching
him from the doorway, commented.

"He is so energetic for a cook. Perhaps that is why he
is not so fat. He must have great pleasure in his cooking
to move so fast."

Richi-Po's white horse was in the stable. He hurried

in past the attendants and, scowling fiercely at them, exclaimed, "A fruitless visit! I must be on my way." They knew what Lotus Blossom looked like and only shrugged their shoulders. Before he could be pursued he was dashing down the road.

It was days later when he finally reported to the Emperor. "I cannot undertake such a mission again, Your Highness. It is full of great danger because many of your people are barbarous. They do not like my courting with a yellow snake. The Princess Lotus Blossom fainted!"

"Too bad," sighed Huang-Ti. "She cannot be the maid I seek." Then he began laughing. "This has been funny."

"Your Highness, since you think this is such a jolly sport, and such happy hunting, why do you not put on my robes and my gold collar and play that you are the matchmaker, and do your own searching for a bride?"

The Emperor stared at him in great surprise. "That is a most preposterous idea!" he exclaimed. "I command you, Richi-Lo, to continue the search for the maid and to devise clever ways to find her."

"If I may take the liberty to say so, it is no more preposterous than wooing a young lady with a snake.

I think unless you yourself find such a one as you are seeking, you may never find her," the matchmaker firmly stated.

"Perhaps you speak wisely," sighed Huang-Ti. "Perhaps I should consider how to begin such a venture."

"But Your Great and Honorable Highness, Your Most Sacred Person, even your poorest subjects do not undertake to find their own brides! No prince, no emperor ever conducted so dreadful a mission as to find himself a bride! Such thinking is too dangerous to contemplate. I am deeply shocked!" The matchmaker promptly fell into a convulsion.

The Emperor tried to revive the poor matchmaker. He was kneeling helplessly beside him when Ta Lo entered the room. Seeing the matchmaker lying on the floor, Ta Lo immediately knew there was something very wrong. He sent for a doctor and took Huang-Ti with him to his private chambers to have a talk with him. Ta Lo didn't ask about what had happened, for he didn't want to embarrass Huang-Ti; he merely suggested that it was time the young man think seriously about his future; he suggested that Huang-Ti go away to school to learn the science of governing China, and that maybe when he returned he would be more ready to take a bride. Huang-Ti, who felt that the matter of finding a bride was becoming very difficult, agreed with Ta Lo's suggestion. And for the next two years, the Emperor was so busily engaged in his studies that he almost forgot about the mysterious young girl he had found in his garden.

8

The Wise Old Man of the River

After Si Ling Chi had climbed back into the tree in her father's yard, she remained seated in the tree considering what she should do next. There was a great commotion below. Her three sisters were talking very loudly and were coming closer. She was able to hear them now, quite clearly.

"We have overlooked much of Si Ling Chi's antics in the past. We have been patient and tolerant beyond the considerations of kindness or need, but when she takes what belongs to another, when she takes our personal belongings, then kindness should end."

"Oh, sister, you would not feel quite so strongly if it were not your ridiculous red pants." It was the younger sister who spoke and made

85

an embarrassed little giggle. "But really, sister, we all consider them beneath the dignity of a lady, especially a fat one."

"If it were not for the beautiful linen cloth that went into their making, I would agree," said the first sister laughing like the cackle of a chicken.

But this laughter filled the second sister with such fury that she looked like she would explode. "You can overlook the serious offense if you like," she shrieked, "but it was not your property she took. I shall beat her within close end of her life."

Si Ling Chi had never had reason to be terrified of her sisters. They often threatened her with dreadful punishment, but children were loved in China and they were seldom punished severely. But her sister whose red pants she had taken had been embarrassed. She had been laughed at, and Si Ling Chi knew that this was very hard to endure. She was really afraid of what this sister might do to her. She was also worried about what her father might do to her when he found out. If the stranger in the garden, who had thought he recognized the jade box, should ask her father about it, or should tell the Emperor, her father might be in disgrace. It was surely unwise for her to come down from the tree. Yes, it was even unwise for her to remain longer in her home. She would have to run away as soon as it was dark. But where would she go? She was not even sure that she could manage to escape. Everyone would be looking for her.

Si Ling Chi stayed in the tree until it was dark, and nobody discovered her. The fancy paper lanterns that decorated the garden at night had burned out. Everything was still and the bough of the tree she was on had become very hard when she finally climbed down. She hurried through the orchard and the vineyard to the low wall that separated the family estate from the hills and the river beyond. She had always wanted to see the river, but her sisters had warned her that a terrible dragon lived there and would surely eat her if he ever caught her on the banks of his river.

She only half believed in the dragon, but half belief had been enough to keep her within sight of her family walls. Now, with the full moon lighting her way, she watched with fast-beating heart until she came in sight of the wide, smooth river. It was dotted with small sailboats on which the river people lived their entire lives.

Si Ling Chi, after looking about at the shadows on the

river bank, decided that none were the shadows of
sleeping dragons or devils, and sat down. The dawn had
begun to reach its fingers across the sky when a small boat
slid so close to the bank that she could easily step aboard.
An old man poled the boat.

"Happy morning," greeted Si Ling Chi. "May I come
on your boat?" The old man looked at her in amazement.

"Who are you?" he asked faintly. "You do not look
like anyone I have ever seen. Are you a good spirit
or a magician?"

"I am Si Ling Chi and have run away from my home.
I am in disgrace. I cannot go back. May I stay on
this boat with you?"

"Come," replied the old man. "I perceive by your
strange clothes, your beauty, and your gentle manner
that you come from some fine family. They will be
greatly concerned when they find you are gone. You may
come on my boat and watch the fishes play in the water
and perhaps learn some new thoughts to think on."
He took Si Ling Chi's hand and helped her into the
boat where she sat upon a low seat beneath a canopy.

"No one will care if I do not return," she said. "I am
only a miserable girl dressed foolishly in my sister's pants

because I wanted a certain moth that lives in the
Emperor's garden. I caught the moth but now I can never
return to my home because I have brought disgrace upon
my father, Ta Lo, who is Chief Counselor to the Emperor."

"Everything and every person has a place and a duty,"
said the old man, who was something of a father and a
priest to the people on the river boats. He helped them
in sickness and in trouble and had grown very wise.
"Why did you want this moth so badly, Si Ling Chi?"

She hurried to show him her collection of bugs and
reptiles. She pulled the jade and sandlewood box out
from under her tunic and handed it to the old man, who
studied it for a long time; then Si Ling Chi opened its
many compartments to show him the creatures she had.

When he returned the box to her he made a deep bow.
"Here is a mystery that I do not understand," he said.
"That box is the most beautiful work of art I have ever
seen. The creatures you have collected in it are symbols
I cannot entirely read, but you are not just a girl,
Si Ling Chi. In some way that no one yet knows, you
are a very special girl. But now it is only important that
I understand what part has been chosen for me to play
in your life. Nothing is a stupid accident. Every person,

every thing fits into a pattern. I must ask the question and try to find a good answer as to why you were waiting on the river bank to come into my small and humble boat."

"Are not some things wrong, some things mistaken in life? Are there really no accidents that are bad, like being born a girl child when your father wants only a son?"

"Ah yes, there are unfortunate happenings. There are cruel errors, but these are not accidents in the perfect pattern. Did you not notice that the white moth had black stripes upon its wings? That would be considered a mistake if a pure white moth were the perfect moth. No, life is not without errors of conduct or judgment, but every error has a lesson if we have the wisdom to learn. One will die without food but the pleasures of eating are increased if one has felt hunger."

Si Ling Chi looked at the old man for a long time. At last she stood up. "You have taught me very much," she said. "Now I shall return to my home and find my duty." Suddenly a new thought came to her. "Perhaps, though, I have come here and found your boat because my duty is to live here with you and be your servant. How can a person know where he belongs in the large pattern of life?"

"What fills us with happiness, what we try to do, what place we are born into, all point the way we will go," said the old man. He smiled. "No, you would not have that beautiful box if you were to be an old man's servant on a fishing boat. The gods would not permit such error. But there is another truth I can tell you about the white moth with black stripes upon its wings. In a monastery where I studied to be a servant of the Great Spirit and all the smaller gods, I learned that the cradles of the baby moths, while they are still like worms, are lined with the softest material ever known to man. I found that these soft linings were very good to put on wounds. At the time, I wondered if these linings could not be put to greater use. I even thought that cloth might be woven from this strange material."

"Thank you, thank you, for a good lesson on your little boat," said Si Ling Chi as she stepped ashore. "I will try to find the pattern of my life and perhaps someday I will also learn the secret of making cloth from the linings of the cradles that the white moths make for their babies."

It was broad daylight when Si Ling Chi arrived back in her own garden. She hid in the shrubs until she was sure her sisters were seated for their morning tea. She then slipped into the sleeping room they all shared; she removed the red trousers and, folding them, laid them deep beneath the other clothing in her middle sister's chest. She made her hair very smooth and piled it high on her head. She put on a yellow robe that had been made for her to wear during the coming Feast of Lanterns. When she had finished making herself as clean and dignified as a young lady could look, she walked with proper little steps into the garden, where her three sisters sat looking tired and worried. Suddenly Si Ling Chi felt like a grown-up young lady and just as suddenly it felt very pleasant to be a grown-up young lady.

Her sisters stared with shocked surprise, but the strong sense of grievance soon loosened the tongue of her middle sister.

"You—you—you wicked girl!" she attempted to shout but fell to coughing.

"Where have you been?" gasped her oldest sister.

"Where are my red trousers?" her middle sister finally managed to demand.

"Why are you so elegantly dressed?" cried the third sister.

Si Ling Chi bowed to her sisters and answered, "A time

comes when a dutiful child must find her proper work.
I think I have found mine, but first I must see my
honorable father." The three sisters were for once
completely speechless.

None of Ta Lo's daughters ever approached their father
without his demanding such an interview. They avoided
any unnecessary meeting with him, but Si Ling Chi was
different. After leaving her sisters, she went to the
chambers her father occupied when he was not at the
palace. She jingled the little bell that hung outside his
door. He was not often here but now he came to the door,
and when he saw that it was his beautiful, youngest
daughter standing before him, he could only stare. In all
China, surely no woman had ever been so bold! But
Si Ling Chi bowed low to her father and said in a soft
voice, "My honorable father, I have a request to make."

"What do you want of me?" asked Ta Lo. "Do I not
provide for every need of my family? Surely, there is
nothing more to ask for."

"Indeed, you provide very well, my father, but I have
learned from a wise man of something that may be of
benefit to all China and I find it my duty to try and learn
more about this thing that is not known."

"I have no time for foolish riddles," said Ta Lo impatiently. "What do you want?"

"Would you permit the gardener to plant many mulberry trees along the garden wall?" asked Si Ling Chi.

"Mulberry trees!" exclaimed Ta Lo. "Why do you want a lot of mulberry trees?"

"It is only on mulberry leaves that the white moth feeds, the white moths that you once told me live in the Emperor's garden. I wish to study the white moths because a wise man has told me that the nests of the young moth worms are lined with the softest covering that has ever been found. Perhaps this could be useful."

Ta Lo just stared at the strange, beautiful girl before him. He seemed to sense that she was someone very special but this left him confused and embarrassed. "Very well," he replied gruffly. "I shall order the gardener to plant a row of mulberry trees." He closed the door abruptly. It certainly was not comfortable to live with such a strange girl, and it was quite disturbing to have her as a part of one's family! He would go back to the palace and his affairs of state, where he felt more certain of things.

9

九

An
Accident
~or a Miracle?

Ta Lo had many mulberry trees
planted in his gardens even though
he thought it quite ridiculous. Now it
was two years later, and the trees
had thrived, and many white moths
with black-striped wings had come
to live on them. Apparently his
youngest daughter was satisfied, for
he had not seen nor heard of her
since that day she had made her
strange request. But then, affairs of
state kept him very busy and he
was not often home.

But if Ta Lo could get back to his
familiar tasks and forget about his
eccentric youngest daughter, her
three sisters could not.

"It was bad enough that she was
interested in all kinds of crawling
things when she was younger, but for
a maid who is almost a woman to be

completely absorbed in worms is not only very disgusting but very unnatural," said the oldest sister.

"And to speak of moths as her little brothers is certainly madness!" said the second sister, who was convinced that Si Ling Chi had strange powers not understood by others. She had certainly made her red trousers appear and disappear in a most unaccountable way. "I think she is a devil. Why do we not stop talking and do something about her?"

"I shall go to the temple and see if the priest will make a horrible mask or something that will frighten the demon out of her," declared the first sister.

"It is only what we should do for own safety," said the third sister.

"We have been protecting her since she was born!" exclaimed the first sister. "Let us now protect ourselves."

"Yes, had we not guarded her very carefully she would have perished long ago," responded the third sister.

"Instead it is we who are in danger of perishing!" exclaimed the second. "She has certainly overcome our father with her tricks. He keeps giving orders for the planting of more and more mulberry trees so her worms can eat and make more and more worms!

Ugh! How horrible it all is!"

"Does this girl you speak of have a father?" asked the priest when the sisters came to him.

"Yes, yes," said the sisters.

"Have her brought to me by her unfortunate parent," ordered the priest.

The sisters left the temple in uncertainty. They had no desire to make their father angry by bringing him into their plans.

"Perhaps declaring Si Ling Chi to be possessed of a demon is not the best plan," said the oldest sister.

"But if we do nothing we shall all have an evil spirit, even our father," said the second. "Then where will China be?"

Perhaps we should try to change Si Ling Chi in another way," suggested the third sister. "Why do we not call in Madam Teng-Teng?"

Madam Teng-Teng was a very important person in the highest social circles of the capital. She was the authority on the proper etiquette for meeting the Emperor, the finest manner of wearing combs in the hair, and the proper way for a young lady to make and pour tea.

"That is a magnificent plan!" cried the second sister, who had always felt cheated because there was never any opportunity for high social functions in Ta Lo's household. "I shall plan at once what I am going to wear."

"We can invite Madam Teng-Teng to come and instruct Si Ling Chi how to make and serve tea," said the oldest sister. "It is something every proper maid should know."

"I shall go and invite her," said the third sister.

"No, no, no!" exclaimed the other two quickly. "We shall all go!"

It was formally arranged with Madam Teng-Teng that she would come and instruct Si Ling Chi how to make and serve tea. At this time Si Ling Chi was using the stone gardenhouse for her workshop, and she spent most of her day scraping the linings from the cocoons, but the piles of soft material were not very useful. The day Madam Teng-Teng was to come, Si Ling Chi was so busy with a new pile which she was trying to dye blue from the juice of a plant that she had quite forgotten the occasion. Her oldest sister was very angry when she had to send a servant to bring Si Ling Chi.

Early on the day that Madam Teng-Teng was to come,

53852

Si Ling Chi's long hair had been arranged high with fancy combs so that there would be less danger of her arriving at the tea party with her hair down her back. But being dressed like an elegant young lady did not distract Si Ling Chi from her fascinating work of unwinding cocoons and trying to dye the soft material. While she was busy with her cocoons, she dropped quite a number of them inside her pocket sleeves, and she forgot to remove them in her hurry to come when summoned.

Making tea was the most ceremonious and social event in Chinese homes. Sometimes it was made in a single large and beautiful teapot. Sometimes it was made in small individual pots. The teapots were among the most beautiful household possessions as were the matching cups from which the tea was sipped.

A large bronze cauldron for boiling water was kept on a metal standard under which oil was burned. While the water boiled and the tea was steeping in the pots, small sweet cakes or fruit were passed among the guests and polite conversation was made or small gossip was carried on. It was considered very important for every woman to know how to conduct a tea party.

When Si Ling Chi entered the parlor, Madam

Teng-Teng was already there. Si Ling Chi had washed her hands and slipped a fresh jacket over her dress. She looked very lovely, and her sisters were pleased to see that after a careful scrutiny by Madam Teng-Teng she met with a nod of approval. The water in the cauldron was boiling and the beautiful tea service was standing on a low table ready for use. The ladies were all seated around it with smiling faces.

"Go fill the teapot, Si Ling Chi, so that everyone can watch you. Bend slightly at the waist and hold your hands gracefully, as if they were two lovely birds," instructed Madam Teng-Teng. She showed her how to hold the teapot. "When you are serving tea, take the smallest steps you can possibly take and still move."

Si Ling Chi took the dipper hanging by the side of the cauldron in her hand. She stooped just a little and paused to allow her sisters and Madam Teng-Teng to admire the full effect as she had been instructed to do. One hand held the lovely porcelain teapot. The other hand was poised over the boiling water delicately holding the dipper. Oh, she is so beautiful, thought her oldest sister. I believe she will grow into a fine lady yet, thought her youngest sister. "Very, very lovely," said Madam

Teng-Teng. But Si Ling Chi had held the pose a
moment too long. The cocoons in her sleeves had
started sliding, sliding down her arm held over the
cauldron. Suddenly there was a splash.

Several things happened at once. Si Ling Chi screamed
and, without hesitating, plunged her hands in the hot
water. The teapot that she dropped shattered into a
thousand pieces. Madam Teng-Teng let out several polite
screeches and scampered to her waiting jinrikisha. The
third sister, who was weeping loudly, picked up the

scattered fragments of the beautiful pot. The second
sister fainted; the oldest came to see what had fallen
into the cauldron and what Si Ling Chi was frantically
picking from it. When she saw, she cuffed the young
girl hard on each cheek.

Of course nobody knew the importance of what was
happening. But when Si Ling Chi hurried to open the
damaged cocoons, the soft linings unwound into a
continuous white thread, very long and very fine.
This was what she had been trying so long to discover

a way to do. She carefully wrapped the thread from each cocoon around her fingers and murmured a happy song under her breath.

"Oh! Oh! Oh! At last I have found the answer! At last I have found the answer! This was what my river boat friend thought could be done with cocoons. This is the happiest day of my life."

Her three sisters regarded her in horrified amazement.

"Look at her!" cried the third sister. "She is completely happy and acts as though something wonderful has taken place when only a disgusting and disgraceful occurrence has utterly ruined the first pleasant social event our household has known since we were born." She turned her face to the wall and moaned bitterly.

"I will not stay under the same roof with her a day longer," wheezed the second, scarcely able to talk above a whisper. "Not one day longer."

"None of us will ever stay under the same roof with her again. Come, we shall put her in the gardenhouse."

"It is too bad," wailed the second. "Though our family has no sons, we have been greatly respected because of our distinguished father, but soon we will become outcasts when people find out that we have a witch

in the family." But her sisters made no move to
approach Si Ling Chi.

She herself decided that it would be best for her project
if she could look after the larvae day and night since it
required endless feeding of mulberry leaves to keep them
alive. They flourished in a constant and warm atmosphere,
so with the help of the old gardener, who had loved her
since she was a small child, she made many box-like
compartments where she could house and feed them
night and day. She made her bed in one corner of the
gardenhouse where the sound of their continuous
munching would have disturbed anyone but a nature lover.

In another small room of the gardenhouse Si Ling Chi
set up the loom she had made. She spent long hours
unwinding and dyeing strands from the cocoons and
weaving the threads into a most beautiful material.
She made her own dyes and colored the material many
shades. The children of the servants had been fascinated
for a long time by Si Ling Chi's activities and now helped
her unwrap the cocoons. Someday this material called
silk would make China famous throughout the world.
Someday men would travel great distances by camel,
by elephant, by horse, and by ship, to buy it from China.

Someday spies would be sent from the surrounding
countries to learn the secret of its preparation, but no
one could foresee these events. Si Ling Chi's sisters
thought she had disgraced them with her worms and
cocoons. They could not forgive her and as time went
on they considered her a menace. At last they decided
to go to the temple and see the high priest once more.

It was a beautiful day when the priest arrived to
take a look at this girl who was supposed to be a witch.
He had never encountered a real witch, but if there
was such an evil person she should be destroyed. At the
request of the sisters and out of curiosity he had come
to the home of Ta Lo.

"Show me the dreadful person," he said to the
three sisters.

They led him to the small house where Si Ling Chi was
absorbed in dyeing some of her cloth a light shade of blue.
She was busy stirring the material in a large kettle and
did not hear them. The children saw them and ran away.

"See how she stirs her evil cauldron just as witches have
always done?" said the oldest sister. The priest entered
very cautiously and looked at the blue material and then
at the beautiful girl, who glanced up at him with startled

eyes. "What are you doing, girl?" he demanded.

"I am making this strange beautiful cloth look like a little of the blue sky," she answered smiling. "Do you not think it is almost as lovely as the sky is happy? I like to think that the walls of heaven are this color."

The priest stumbled back, looking first at the girl and then at the material. "She is not a witch! She is not even a girl! She is a goddess!"

10

The Emperor Finds His Bride

The two years the Emperor had been away at school had passed quickly for him. He had learned many important things about how to govern his country and his people so that they could continue to live happily and peacefully. Now he was home again and the problem of finding a bride was still upon him. Ta Lo was becoming very insistent about it, for a young Emperor had to have a wife so he could bring a fine heir into the world.

Huang-Ti spent many hours in his garden, brooding about his future. One day soon after his return, as he was gazing up at the sky through the leaves of a mulberry tree, a white moth with black stripes on its wings flew by. Without thinking, the Emperor reached out and caught it.

He looked at it a long time as it struggled to escape.
Then he saw on its fluttering wings, as if in a dream, the
beautiful face of the strange girl he had caught and lost.
He remembered her interest in the moths. "You are a
puzzle, my little brother. What is it about you that so
intrigued the girl I want to marry? For it is she, and only
she, who can fill the place in the scheme of my fate. But
where is she? Where did she come from? Where did she
disappear to so quickly? Surely she must live some place
close by. Even a nymph must live close to her playground.

"Perhaps. . . ." He glanced up and saw a corner of the
wall that separated his estates from Ta Lo's. "Perhaps she
lives in Ta Lo's gardens. . . ." Suddenly he jumped up in
his excitement. "Yes! Yes! I think that is the way it is!
I think the jade box that she kept her pets in is like the
jade box I once gave to Ta Lo when his son was to have
been born!" He hurried into the royal chambers and
had Richi-Po summoned.

While waiting for Richi-Po the Emperor strode
anxiously around his room. He remembered what had
happened the last time Richi-Po had helped him and he
was afraid the matchmaker would not come. But Richi-Po
came, for he loved his willful Emperor. Also, he hoped

that in these past two years of growth and learning, the
Emperor had forgotten his foolish dreams of youth and
now wanted his matchmaker to seek a wife in the
traditional manner. When he arrived, Huang-Ti
wasted no time in telling him of his new project.

"Dear friend," began the Emperor. "I know that I gave
you a difficult and wearisome task when I asked you to
take that box and its contents to all the maids in the
kingdom. However, there is one girl who I am sure is
the one I am seeking. Please go on one more errand
with the jade box and yellow snake. And if you
cannot find her this time, then you need never
go on such an errand again."

The matchmaker, who usually loved his work and
treasured his high position, put his head on his arm and
wept. "Your Highness, I was still a fairly young man
without a white hair when I first answered your summons,
but now I have grown old and feel more white hairs
sprouting every minute. How can I do as you ask,
yet how can I refuse such a sweet Emperor?"

"I do not ask you to travel far this time," said Huang-Ti.
"You have only to travel beyond my walls to the household

of my Chief Counselor, Ta Lo. I believe you will find the maiden I am seeking there."

"Ta Lo?" repeated the surprised matchmaker. "Ta Lo has three ugly daughters no longer young, for whom I have never been able to make a match. Who in this household could possibly become the Empress, My Young Lord?"

"I do not know, but I think you will find such a one there. Perhaps she is a nymph. Perhaps a sprite. She may be a servant. But find her and make the proper arrangements for marriage."

That same day Richi-Po's elaborate sedan chair stopped before the gate of Ta Lo's household. An astonished group of people watched from the windows and doorways to see this important person arrive.

The commotion started with the gardener. He opened the gates wide and bowed, then fled to the house where he stuttered his news so badly that the servant to whom he spoke could hardly understand what he was saying. When he did, he in turn ran, shouting, "Richi-Po! Richi-Po, the matchmaker, has at last arrived at the honorable home of Ta Lo!"

The three sisters heard and turned pale, then red.

The oldest ran for her mirror and stared into it gloomily.
The second pulled out her bed roll and sank upon it,
wheezing alarmingly. The third hurried as fast as her
small feet would carry her to put on her most
elaborate gown and set large combs in her hair.

The matchmaker was at last invited in and was shown
to the parlor with his servant, who carried the facsimile
of the jade box.

"I wish to see all the young women of this household,"
said Richi-Po. "I wish to interview all, even servants.
I am here in the name of the Emperor. No one
is to be overlooked."

The women of Ta Lo's household were assembled.
Then the unmarried were separted from the married.
All were present except Si Ling Chi, who was busily
working in the gardenhouse, weaving and embroidering,
unaware of what was going on at the big house.

When Richi-Po's manservant brought forth the jade
box, the three sisters could not help but exclaim,
"Father's jade box!"

"If it is not his, it is one exactly like it!"
croaked the oldest.

"It is like the one the Emperor gave him!" whistled the second, gasping for breath.

"It is just like the one he gave Si Ling Chi, but I am sure it is still with her night and day!" cried the third.

"Where is this Si Ling Chi?" asked the matchmaker.

"You could not possibly want to see her. She is hardly a woman or a girl. She is a witch who lives in the gardenhouse .

"She is very, very dreadful!" added the second sister.

"She is to be feared and avoided," said the third. "She is a disgrace to the honorable family of Ta Lo."

"One thing more," said Richi-Po in a voice of authority. "You must each look at the contents of this jade box. It is a command of the Emperor."

After he showed each girl or woman the yellow snake, there was never time to show the white and black moths. They went away screaming or they fainted. The three sisters backed away, and the oldest one said, "This reminds me of the time we tried to get the jade box from Si Ling Chi."

"Take me to this creature you call Si Ling Chi," commanded Richi-Po.

The three sisters, followed by all the household servants, led him out to the gardens in the back, out to the stone gardenhouse where Si Ling Chi sat cross-legged, sewing and singing one of her happy songs.

Meanwhile, Ta Lo's chair was being carried along the road leading to his home. Ta Lo was returning from a long trip. He had gone to a far province to interview the chief family in hopes of finding a daughter the Emperor would be willing to marry. He had found that the only marriageable daughter was an ambitious widow who was ten years older than the Emperor and had two sons. He knew that the stubborn young Emperor would never marry such a woman, so he had left for home immediately. Therefore he was very tired and discouraged when his chair finally came to a stop before the door of his house. In fact, he was so tired he did not even notice the elegant sedan chair of the matchmaker.

Whenever Ta Lo entered his house after having been gone for many days, a manservant would run out and remove his shoes, prepare his bath, and bring him tea. But this time no one came, not even when he rang the little string of musical bells that hung by the entrance.

He went to his own private chambers, meeting no one
on the way. He passed through the house and walked out
into his garden. Then he saw the excited and concentrated
crowd around the gardenhouse. Had there been a
disaster, an earthquake? What could this strange hubbub
mean? He hurried over and pushed through the absorbed
assembly, which did not even realize he was there.
In the foreground were his three older daughters and
the matchmaker. And who was the beautiful. . . . Could
it be. . . . Yes, it was his youngest daughter, Si Ling Chi.
In one hand she held the jade box and in the other a
little yellow snake. He was just in time to hear Richi-Po
ask, "What is your name, young lady?"

"I am Si Ling Chi, youngest daughter of Ta Lo,
Chief Counselor to the Emperor," she replied.

"What is all this about?" demanded Ta Lo. "Has the
girl done something to cause a scandal in my household?"

The matchmaker turned around and saw Ta Lo for the
first time. "Greetings, Ta Lo," he said and bowed. "This
young lady certainly will cause news, but I do not think
it could be called a scandal. It seems that our young
Emperor knows something about her, though how, I have

not the least idea. He gave me this jade box containing a yellow snake and several moths and told me to find the one who would recognize the box and not be afraid of the snake. He said when I found such a girl, she would know the special meaning of the moths. Ta Lo, your daughter fits this description. She is beautiful, as you can see. She claims this jade box is somewhat like one she has, and look for yourself at the magic she has performed with the aid of the black and white moths." Richi-Po made a wide gesture toward several rolls of beautiful cloth. "She is either a witch or a goddess, and in either case, the Emperor has sent me to make arrangements for his marriage to her."

"Marriage?" muttered Ta Lo. "The Emperor wishes to arrange a marriage to my daughter, Si Ling Chi?"

"Yes," answered the matchmaker, anxious to conclude the tiresome business before this mysterious girl could disappear again or the Emperor change his mind.

11

十一

A Prophecy Comes True

The sudden reversal of her family's attitude toward her was very confusing to Si Ling Chi. Why did the Emperor want to marry her? Why had he sent the matchmaker with the imitation jade box and the yellow snake? How could he know how important the black and white moths were to her? She was certain that she had never seen the Emperor and that he had never seen her. He, too, must think that she was a witch and he only wanted to marry her so he could punish her. He had absolute authority over everyone and was to be feared more than the stern-looking priest who had come several times with her sisters to see her. Then she remembered the young man who had helped her catch the moths in the Emperor's garden.

118

He must have been the Emperor's bodyguard. He must have told the Emperor about the ridiculous and stupid girl who had climbed over his wall and tried to pass as a boy.

She had never been frightened by stories of dragons or wild animals, but she was frightened of this Emperor whom she had never seen. She was sure he wanted to make her suffer for her audacity. Or perhaps he would shut her in his tower and try to make her spin the silk from the cocoons into gold. Even her father had said, "Si Ling Chi, this discovery of yours will no doubt bring great riches to China. We can turn this beautiful material into gold for our coffers." Si Ling Chi had stared at him in amazement then. But now she was quite frightened by the whole idea since the matchmaker had come to make arrangements for her marriage to the Emperor.

There was just one task she wished to complete before she left her home. She wanted to present a gift to that young man who had helped her catch the black and white moths in the Emperor's garden. She spent days dyeing silk to make a coat for him. In green and gold thread she embroidered a gorgeous dragon with a very long winding tail across the back of it.

But although Si Ling Chi's heart grew heavier as the

wedding approached, her sisters were happier than they had ever been. They could not in the least understand how Si Ling Chi had succeeded in casting her witch's spell over the Emperor without even seeing him, but for once her strange power was bringing honor and excitement to their secluded household. Gifts were arriving by the chestsful. Splendid horses were sent to Ta Lo. Dressmakers arrived to make them beautiful gowns and shoes. Articles made from costly jade, precious stones, and pearls arrived. Special cooks came to make elaborate cakes for the wedding feast. Jeweled combs and collars were designed for each of them. The sisters were so occupied they did not see how pale and thin Si Ling Chi had grown. How could they know that she was trying to gather the courage to escape before this dreadful thing could happen to her. She would try to get back to the river boat where the old man lived. This time he might let her stay with him.

But Si Ling Chi found no chance to run away. In fact the Emperor had insisted that Ta Lo have his house better guarded since the future Empress of China now lived there. The guards only convinced Si Ling Chi that she was indeed a prisoner.

At last the day of the wedding arrived and preparations

were started at dawn. To begin as the sun was coming up
was considered to be lucky and to add to the happy
prospects for a long and fortunate marriage. The bride
was required to spend an hour before the household gods,
asking for proper humility before her husband, that her
marriage be blessed with many sons, and that the Emperor
have a long life. Instead, Si Ling Chi asked the god
Shoku-Po, who had allowed her, many years ago, to hold
the great pearl from his forehead for a whole day, to help
her now. She asked that she find some joy to bear her
long imprisonment in the Emperor's royal prison. She
could not help weeping and was glad no one saw her.
Finally she left the family shrine and went to her sisters'
chambers, where she was to be dressed by them for her
wedding. They were discussing her as she approached.

"Si Ling Chi is so quiet," said the younger sister.
"Never since the day she was born has she been so docile."

"I have noticed," replied the middle sister. "It alarms
me because this is not normal and when Si Ling Chi
is not acting normal we know by now to expect
some catastrophe."

"I think for once she is frightened," said the oldest
sister. "And I think I too would be frightened. Emperor

Huang-Ti is reported to be an unusual person and that would be more than a little alarming. Of course," she continued thoughtfully, "if he were not so he would never have wanted to marry Si Ling Chi, but I think it would be terrifying to marry any kind of Emperor!"

The three sisters stopped talking as Si Ling Chi came forward. They guided her to her bath and then brought out the traditional linen undergarments of a bride. Si Ling Chi pushed them aside and brought out some undergarments she had made herself. This brought forth a storm of protests from her sisters.

"Si Ling Chi! You are not going to be married in that stuff made by worms, are you?" demanded the younger.

"Of course she is, sister," said the second with great sarcasm. "Don't you know by now that the little worms are her relatives, her little brothers? Why wear linen made from a plant if you can have a magic robe made by worms!"

"It *is* very beautiful, sisters," said the oldest. "We have been hard to convince, but truly, there has never been a more beautiful material than this that Si Ling Chi with her moths has made. She deserves to be Empress."

"Thank you, sister! Thank you!" said Si Ling Chi bowing. "I am pleased that you find my cloth beautiful.

When I wear it I feel that I have dressed myself in a
lovely song, a song made from a gentle breeze blown
over a flower garden. But today it does not feel that way
to me. Today I am frightened." Si Ling Chi sank to the
floor, weeping. The three sisters looked at her in
consternation. Never before had they seen her
so frightened and unhappy.

"Do not be frightened, Si Ling Chi. The Emperor is
called Heavenly One. He is reported to be young and not
bound by chains of old tradition," counseled her older
sister. "Come, put on this beautiful sky-colored gown you
have woven and sewn for yourself. I will arrange the veil
so that you cannot see your bridegroom, and so that he
cannot see you until after the wedding. He too will have
his face covered, Si Ling Chi, until after you are married.
It is considered bad luck for a bride or a groom to see each
other for the first time until after they are married and
alone." Si Ling Chi allowed herself to be dressed and her
long hair to be piled high and held with golden combs.

A golden sedan chair with a canopy and drawn curtains
arrived on the shoulders of four liveried men to take
Si Ling Chi to the palace. She had skillfully concealed
within her long sleeves the crimson robe she intended to

give the young man she had met in the Emperor's garden, the young man who had made this discovery possible. She had not seen him since that day, but she wanted him to have this gift made from the wonderful cloth.

Ta Lo followed in his own handsome horse-drawn carriage. The three sisters, looking impressive if not beautiful, followed in a special jinrikisha.

The ceremony was long but quite simple. A large golden bowl filled with rice was passed from the Emperor after he had eaten from it, to Si Ling Chi. A priest lifted the bride's veil just enough to permit her to eat a little rice and sip a little wine from the large silver cup. The bowl and cup then passed, first to all members of both families and then to all the guests. Various food courses were then served with much wine. After three hours of this, the guests were in a merry mood, and as members of both families mingled, talking and exchanging gifts according to the traditional manner, Si Ling Chi was able to slip away to the garden. The Emperor removed his veil and looked for his bride to lift hers, but he couldn't find her anywhere. He decided to go into the garden for a breath of fresh air.

He went to a corner of the garden far from the

festivities, where the only sounds were the rustle of leaves and the scolding of birds. As he sat down on a bench, he removed his ceremonial robe. "Marriage is an uncomfortable custom," he muttered. "I want only to see my bride but all this feasting and talking goes on and on. And this accepting of gifts in proper order is endless! And now my bride has disappeared!" The Emperor closed his eyes. Suddenly he was startled by someone from behind.

"I am so happy to find you still in the Emperor's garden," laughed Si Ling Chi. "I never learned who you are, but it seems only right and proper that you who helped me catch the moths should have a gift made of their cloth." She brought out the beautiful flame-colored gown with the green and gold dragon embroidered on it. "You no doubt have heard that I have married the Emperor, Huang-Ti. Now I must return to be unveiled by my groom."

"Not so fast, Si Ling Chi. You escaped me once and it has taken many seasons of searching to find you! I do not intend to let you get away again."

"You—you—you must be. . . . You are the Emperor!" gasped Si Ling Chi.

"Yes and indeed!" laughed Huang-Ti, jumping to his feet. He first removed her veil and then accepted the scarlet robe. "And what do I do with a bride who runs out on her own wedding before she is unveiled to give such a gorgeous gift to an unknown man?" He put on the robe.

"You take her back to the guests and behave like a proper bridegroom and Emperor," said Si Ling Chi pertly.

The Emperor laughed to find that his bride was still as impudent as she had been that day long ago in his garden. He took her by the arm and led her back to where the guests and members of the family were still celebrating. Ta Lo came over to them and exclaimed over the crimson robe the Emperor was wearing.

"It is a gift from my bride," said Huang-Ti.

Others, attracted by the vivid colors of the robe, came over to congratulate the happy pair.

"What name shall we give to this beautiful material?" Ta Lo asked.

"Since it was discovered and perfected by my Empress, we shall call it by her name—Si!" proudly replied Huang-Ti.

As everyone crowded round them, they heard the joyous ringing of a great bell. Ta Lo had ordered the golden bell of his wonderful child to be rung, for Poco Shan's prophecy of eighteen years ago was now fulfilled.

GERTRUDE WEAVER has written many short stories for children, but this is her first book-length story. Totally disabled by multiple sclerosis, except for the use of her head, she has been able—with a pointer between her teeth and an electric typewriter—to create poems, stories, and plays.

The inspiration for *The Emperor's Gift* was the legend of the discovery of silk in China about 2700 B.C. So little is known of this ancient period that Mrs. Weaver chose as the setting for this historical fantasy the era of Pearl Buck's *The Good Earth* because it gave her "a real sense of China."

A major in sociology at Ohio Wesleyan University, she did settlement work with children at Eli Bates House in Chicago. Being the mother of four children and a foster mother to many others, her main interest has continued to be working with young people. While living in the Cleveland area she was active in the dramatic arts, presenting programs in the schools. Later a nursery school she began in her home in Columbus, Ohio, became the Maple Grove Nursery School, which continues with new methods of beginning education. In Grand Rapids, Michigan, where she now lives, she has worked with children, in spite of her disability, tutoring, presenting plays, operating a day-care center, and writing stories.

UNADA, the illustrator for this book, graduated from the College of Fine Arts of Syracuse University. After varied experience in advertising, lithography, fashion design, and publishing, she decided to free-lance. In little more than a year in her Philadelphia studio she has created the illustrations for eight books for children including *Saucy, Trading Post Girl,* and *Sequoya.*